Little Blue Eyes

Avon Books are available at special quantity discounts for bulk purchases for sales promotions, premiums, fund raising or educational use. Special books, or book excerpts, can also be created to fit specific needs.

For details write or telephone the office of the Director of Special Markets, Avon Books, Dept. FP, 1350 Avenue of the Americas, New York, New York 10019, 1-800-238-0658.

Little Blue Eyes

LOIS SZYMANSKI

Illustrated by Doron Ben-Ami

AN AVON CAMELOT BOOK

VISIT OUR WEBSITE AT
http://AvonBooks.com

LITTLE BLUE EYES is an original publication of Avon Books. This work has never before appeared in book form.

AVON BOOKS
A division of
The Hearst Corporation
1350 Avenue of the Americas
New York, New York 10019

Copyright © 1997 by Lois Knight Szymanski
Illustrations copyright © 1997 by Avon Books
Interior illustrations by Doron Ben-Ami
Published by arrangement with the author
Library of Congress Catalog Card Number: 96-96917
ISBN: 0-380-78487-4
RL: 3.0

First Avon Camelot Printing: February 1997

CAMELOT TRADEMARK REG. U.S. PAT. OFF. AND IN OTHER COUNTRIES, MARCA REGISTRADA, HECHO EN U.S.A.

Printed in the U.S.A.

OPM 10 9 8 7 6 5 4 3 2 1

This book is dedicated to my daughter, Ashley,
whose enthusiasm and excitement
is contagious, igniting the fires of imagination.

1

Meg sat cross-legged on a bale of straw. She waited in the feed room beside her pony's stall with her head in her hands, her elbows propped on her knees. Her long, brown hair fell across her face, covering the smattering of freckles that arched across her upturned nose. The straw scratched her legs just below the hem of her shorts, so she wiggled to get more comfortable. She hadn't been this worried since last spring, when Foxy had jumped the fence and disappeared across the meadow and up the mountainside.

Now, Meg heard Dr. Shura talking to Dad on the other side of the wall. She pressed her face against the rough lumber planks and peered through a crack to try to see what was going on in Foxy's stall. Dr. Shura was removing a rubber glove from her hand. She grinned at Dad as she spoke. Her head bobbed up and down, and her long, red curls bounced with every word. But Dad didn't smile back. He shook his head, a shocked expression on his face.

Meg sat back and sighed. She'd hated being told to wait outside. After all, the mare had belonged to her for most of her ten years. Foxy was *her* pony! But Dr. Shura had said that too many people in the stall during the examination would get the pony worked up. The next thing Meg knew, she was waiting alone in the room next door.

Meg dropped a leg over the side of the bale and began impatiently drumming her heel against the straw. She thought about last spring when Foxy had leapt the fence and galloped across the meadow, her head held high, her tail waving in the wind. Foxy had streaked up the face of Sidling Mountain without even looking back. In the evening sun, her coat had reflected shiny red, the color of a fall apple, the color of fox-fire.

Meg remembered the empty feeling she'd had in the pit of her stomach as the mare had become a dot in the distance, and how she had felt even worse with each passing day. It had been a week before a friend just over the mountain in Buck Valley had called to say that he had her pony in his barn. He'd found her on the mountaintop and she had come to him willingly.

Foxy came home with a mane and tail that were tangled and full of burrs. She also came home a different pony. She was calmer and kinder than she had ever been before the wild escape.

Looking back, Meg realized she'd thought the worst was over. She told herself that as long as Foxy didn't escape again, things would be fine. She had checked and rechecked the gates and kept a close eye on Foxy, but the pony now seemed uninterested in jumping fences. So things should have been fine. But they weren't!

Over the months, the little red mare went from calm to just plain lethargic. She lost all of her energy and spent hours, daily, lying in the sun, soaking up the heat, unmoving. Then she began to gain weight like crazy. Now, just ten months after her escape, Foxy looked like a balloon about to burst.

Meg twirled a curl around her fingertip and bumped her foot against the bale again. Her stomach churned as she waited for the veterinarian to come out of the stall with her father. *What was wrong with her pony? And what was taking them so long?*

Just when Meg thought she would have to get up and march into the stall next door to demand an answer, she heard Dr. Shura and Dad coming out.

"But I don't understand how this could have happened," Dad was saying.

"Well, certainly she must have had contact with another pony," Dr. Shura said. "When was she in the company of other horses?"

"I don't know . . ." Dad answered thoughtfully.

Meg met them in the aisle. "What is it?" she asked. "What's wrong with Foxy?"

Dad didn't seem to hear Meg. He was staring at Dr. Shura as they walked down the long barn aisle and out into the sunshine. "There was that time when she escaped. It was ten, no, almost eleven months ago. Who knows what she may have found on her adventure?"

"Dad!" Meg yanked on her father's elbow to get his attention. She was beginning to panic. "Did Foxy catch a disease or something from another pony? What is wrong with her?"

Dad stopped, the dazed look draining from his face. "I'm sorry, honey," he said. "Nothing is wrong with your pony," he said. "She'll be just fine."

"But she's so fat and lazy now," Meg said.

"Well, Megan," Dr. Shura said, a smile spreading across her face. "You would be fat and tired too, if you were about to have a foal, like Foxy is!"

Meg stopped in her tracks. Daddy and

Dr. Shura stopped too, smiling down at her.

"Foxy is going to have a foal?" Meg asked with wonder in her voice. Then, "My pony is going to have a baby!" The second time, she shrieked the words at the top of her lungs. Spinning in her tracks, she bolted back into the barn and down the cool aisle to Foxy's stall. She slid open the bolt on the door and slipped inside.

"Hey, Foxy! How are you doing? You're going to have a foal! How about that, girl?"

Meg wrapped her arms around the pony's neck and hugged her tight. Foxy stood quietly. With big brown eyes, she gazed deep into Meg's equally brown eyes. She blinked, her long lashes brushing together, then opened her eyes to look at Meg again. It was as if the pony could read Meg's thoughts, as if she could feel Meg's joy. Meg stared back, spellbound, surprised at the level of understanding that seemed to pass between them.

The spell was broken when Foxy

reached down to nibble on the hay at her feet. Meg fluffed the bushy mane, running her fingers through thick strands. Then she let her hand drop, to slide it over the bulging belly. She touched Foxy's soft, red hair with gentle fingertips, rubbing over the round form inside.

That night Meg knelt by her bedroom windowsill and watched Foxy. Moonlight spilled across the pasture, washing it with soft, yellow light. Foxy was grazing, cropping grass with strong, white teeth, stepping slowly from patch to patch of green. Her coat reflected the light just like the fox-fire plant she drew her name from. Suddenly, she threw her head up. Ears pricked, she stared into the trees at the top of Sidling Mountain. Her body quivered and she let out a long and mournful whinny.

Meg shivered as she watched Foxy return to her grazing. *What had she heard on the mountaintop?* Meg wondered. Meg backed away from the window and the

curtains fell forward again. Catching the evening breeze, they billowed out. Meg crawled into bed and settled herself under the covers. She closed her eyes as Foxy's whinny echoed in the night.

2

That night, ponies pranced in Meg's dream, red ponies with flowing manes and tails, and deep, liquid brown eyes. Each of them had a bright star in the center of its forehead, just like Foxy had, but unlike Foxy, these ponies glowed fluorescent in the night, as bright as fox-fire on the trees. Yet one of the ponies in Meg's dream was pure white, and its magic was full of light and good. When Meg looked into its eyes, she felt as if she and the white pony were speaking without words.

In the morning, Meg awoke with a start. Her dream had been so real that it took the morning light, great gulps of air,

and plenty of eye-rubbing to bring her back to her bedroom, to make her believe that it had been just that, a dream.

She dressed slowly, remembering the red ponies that looked like Foxy, and the pure white one, remembering how magical they had seemed. Magical. The word stuck in her mind and her thoughts fell on the pure white pony. It had known her.

Meg rubbed her face vigorously with both hands. *This is silly,* she thought. *It was just a dream!* But she smiled just the same, because the dream had been a good one.

Downstairs, Meg poured herself a bowl of cereal.

"Hey, Meggie! What do you have planned for this beautiful summer Saturday?" Mom swept her way down the hallway and into the kitchen, brandishing the broom as if sweeping floors was fun.

"I thought I'd fool around with Foxy. Groom her. Clean her stall. That kind of stuff." Meg poured milk over her Crunchios and stuffed a spoonful into her mouth.

Mom leaned on the broom handle and rolled her eyes. "I can't believe that pony of yours," she said. "Went out and found herself a boyfriend last year . . . Who'd have thought?"

As Mom's voice trailed off, Meg munched her cereal. "She sure kept it a secret."

"She's still keeping it a secret," Mom said. A smile played at the corner of her lips. "I just wonder what the stallion looks like," she added softly.

Meg lifted her bowl and slurped down the last of the cereal and milk. "Me too," she answered, wondering what color the father of the foal was.

Foxy was lying on her side under the big apple tree. Thick white blossoms drifted down, landing all about her. They were as pure white as the pony in Meg's dream. Now, the blossoms covered Foxy's heaving body with a blanket of white.

Meg stood beside her sleeping pony. She watched the mare's bulging side rise and fall with the even breaths of sleep.

"Hey, Foxy!" Meg whispered. "Are you going to sleep all day?"

Foxy's eyes fluttered open slowly, and she raised her head to gaze at Meg. Once again, Meg felt as if the pony were speaking through her eyes. It was as if Foxy were saying, "Good morning, Meg. I'll be up in just a moment."

Meg giggled, and the red mare scrambled to her feet and shook the blossoms from her fiery coat.

"You sure have gotten slow these days," Meg teased the mare. Wrapping an arm around Foxy's neck, she walked to the barn with her pony. "I never could have crept up on you like that before," she said. "Before you were with foal, you would have heard the back door slam!"

Foxy stopped and turned a slow gaze on Meg, reaching out to rub a whiskery muzzle over Meg's cheek, then began walking again. Meg stared at the mare in amazement.

She released Foxy and followed her swishing tail the rest of the way to the barn. "This is crazy," she said out loud.

"I'm letting that silly dream get to me, that's what I'm doing. Just because my pony looks at me or nuzzles me, I think she's talking! Geez! This is silly!"

Meg groomed Foxy until her coat glistened in the afternoon sun. She ran two buckets full of water, and placed them just outside of the stall door. She scooped a measure of grain into the food bin, lay down fresh straw, and filled the hay bag to the top. By the time she went inside for lunch, Foxy was asleep again, this time on the fresh, yellow straw inside her stall. Meg began to worry. *Is it normal for a pony to sleep so much when she is pregnant?* she wondered.

On Friday, Meg wandered down the winding path that led through the forest behind Foxy's pasture. She couldn't wait to tell Mrs. Storm that Foxy was pregnant. Mrs. Storm and Meg had been friends for years. The older woman's love for animals and nature had always fascinated Meg, who had learned from Mrs. Storm how to feed the squirrels and birds in the winter and put out apples for the deer in the summer.

There were many times that Meg had wished a kid just her age would move in nearby. But they lived in the country, so Meg counted herself lucky that she did have Mrs. Storm. During the school year, she sometimes felt guilty, because school friends kept her busy and she didn't visit Mrs. Storm as often.

Today, Meg was happy and carefree. It was finally summer, she hadn't seen Mrs. Storm in a while, and she had news to share. It had been a week since she'd found out that a foal was on the way. But the last days of school had kept her busy. At last, she could visit!

Meg ducked under a large, silvery web that stretched across the path from a thin sapling to a tangle of raspberry bushes. As she passed under the web, a dark, leggy spider skittered sideways, then slipped silently down a silky strand and out of sight. When Meg straightened, she could see Mrs. Storm's cottage just ahead. It was tiny, but neat. It sat among the trees and bushes, surrounded by flowers and tangled wildlife. The windows were dark and the shades were drawn.

Meg hurried down the path. Something was not right. Mrs. Storm always raised her shades first thing in the morning. By now, she should have been outside, puttering in her garden or sketching pictures on paper clipped to the easel she liked to set up in the garden.

After she rapped on the door, Meg leaned close. She heard a voice call out weakly, "Come in."

Worried, Meg opened the door.

3

"Come in, Meg," Mrs. Storm called softly.

Meg entered the room, closing the door behind her.

It took Meg's eyes a moment to adjust to the dark inside. Then she saw Mrs. Storm curled up on her sofa, covered with an afghan. "Are you sick, Mrs. Storm?" she asked.

"Oh, I've come down with a bug, all right," Mrs. Storm said. "But I'll be fine in a few days."

Brushing a strand of dark brown hair from her face, Meg sat on the end of the sofa by Mrs. Storm's feet. She didn't like the raspy sound that came from Mrs. Storm's chest when she breathed, or the

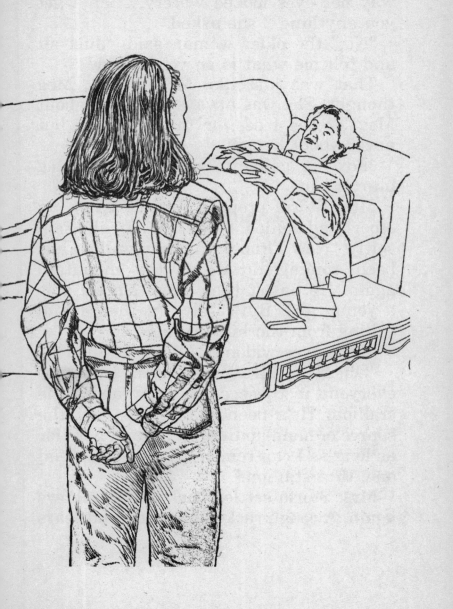

way her eyes looked watery. "Can I get you anything?" she asked.

"No," the older woman said. "Just sit and tell me what is on your mind."

That was just like Mrs. Storm, Meg thought. She was always worrying about Meg, or the trees, or the squirrels, but never about herself.

"Foxy is going to have a foal," Meg blurted out.

Mrs. Storm propped herself up on an elbow and smiled. "Well, I'll be," she said softly. "Now I know why that stallion has been coming down off the mountain again. He hasn't been down since I was a young girl. But lately, I've heard him calling from the hills at night."

Meg's eyes widened. "What stallion?"

"Oh, Meg," Mrs. Storm said. "I thought everyone in these parts knew about the stallion. He's been a mystery, and the source of hand-spun tales around here for as long as I can remember. He's a special one, that stallion."

Mrs. Storm settled back on the pillows again. A cough racked her body and tears came to her eyes. "I used to put apples out for him when I was a young girl, just so I could see him come down at night. Yes, he was magnificent! He and I became fast friends." Mrs. Storm paused, looking thoughtful. "I miss seeing him. Oh, what a wonderful white giant he was!"

Meg gasped.

"What is it, love?"

"Nothing, really," Meg said. "It's just that I dreamed of a white pony stallion. He was tall and mysterious, and there was something magical about him."

Mrs. Storm smiled knowingly. She pulled the afghan up to her chin and closed her eyes. Then she fell silent.

"Mrs. Storm?" Meg leaned closer. "Are you asleep?"

Mrs. Storm opened an eye and gave a tiny smile. "Not yet," she said. "But maybe you should let me rest for a while, love."

Meg let herself out the door she had come in. She walked slowly down the path, absorbed in thought. Mrs. Storm

21

never got sick. She was always full of energy, bubbling with fun and adventure. Meg thought of the white stallion. Had she dreamed of him for a reason? Was he too old to be the father of Foxy's unborn foal? Or could the foal be his?

Meg wandered through the forest, not even noticing the spider or the web, or the way the sunlight filtered through the trees and danced in patterns on the ground. She'd only been away from home for an hour, but Meg, weighed down with worries, felt as though the time had stretched into hours. She was still lost in thought when she slipped between the bars of the fence into Foxy's pasture.

She saw Dad waving his arms and calling. At first, she couldn't understand what he was saying. But as she drew closer, his voice became more clear and her heart jumped in her throat.

"Come quick!" he said. "Foxy has just had her foal!"

4

Foxy was on her side, her back to Meg.
She turned her head, watching as Meg,
Mom, and Dad approached. Her eyes met
Meg's and she lowered her lashes, almost
bashfully. Then she turned her attention
to the front again.

Meg moved around the mare slowly so
she wouldn't startle the new mother. She
needn't have worried, though. Foxy's attention was now on the tiny, white bundle that rested in the warm curve of
her body.

Pure white, the foal was thin and awk-
ward in appearance. Its head appeared
too big for its body and its legs were long
and knobby-kneed. If Meg didn't already

know that this was the way a foal was supposed to look, she would have been worried. But knowing what she did, she just smiled at the jumble of delicate angles, marveling at the bright of the white and the thickness of the dark lashes that fringed the eyes.

Meg fell to her knees in front of the mare and her newborn. Cautiously, she reached out to touch the baby, and a rush of emotions overcame her. Meg had only found out a week ago that her mare would have a foal, and now here it was, so small and soft and beautiful.

Its eyes fluttered open and Meg gasped as the foal stared into her own eyes. It wasn't just the intensity of the newborn's gaze that had jarred her so, but the color, too. The eyes were blue, a crystal clear, glassy, lake-blue, and they seemed to look right into her soul . . . to read her thoughts as Foxy had done over the past few days.

"Would you look at those eyes," Mom said softly. "Clear blue . . ."

Meg smiled up at her dad. "Is it a boy or a girl?" she asked.

"Boy," Dad said, and a smile spread across his face. "You have yourself a colt, Meggie."

Meg turned back to the pony, tuning out everything else. The newborn's hair was thick and pure. Its hooves were light tan, almost yellow. Each nostril flared slightly, soft and pink, whuffing in the smells of a new world. Then there were those eyes . . . those incredible blue eyes. They were the shade of blue she had used to paint a seascape in her art class last semester. What was that shade called? Then she remembered.

"Is azure a shade of blue?" Meg asked her mom suddenly.

"Yes," Mom said, startled. "Almost the same shade of blue as his eyes!"

Meg stroked the foal's neck, then ran a finger around the whorl of hair on his forehead. "That's his name," she said. "His name is Azure."

She didn't look to see what they thought of the name. Instead, Meg's eyes flickered from Foxy to the foal, then back to the mare again and again.

Foxy watched Meg with a softness Meg had never noticed before. Pure contentment seemed to have washed over her. *Look at my foal,* Foxy told Meg with her eyes. *Look at my perfect baby boy.*

That night Meg slept fitfully. The dreams of magical horses came to her again and she heard a stallion calling from the mountaintop. When she awoke, Meg wondered if the dreams were truly dreams. They had seemed so real. Especially the sound of the whinny that had rippled down from the mountaintop.

5

Soon it was Monday. Meg skipped down the forest path, slowing only to duck under the web and continue on her way. She was bursting with happiness over the new colt, and she knew that Mrs. Storm would be excited too, especially when she heard that the colt was white! Meg slowed as she came to the clearing around Mrs. Storm's cottage. She smiled to herself as she crossed the grassy lawn. Suppose the white stallion on the mountain was the colt's father? That would make Meg's pony part of a legend, wouldn't it?

When Meg stepped up to the porch and rapped on the door, silence greeted her.

She pressed her ear to the wooden door, but she couldn't hear any movement inside the house. Should she just go inside, she wondered? What if Mrs. Storm was even sicker? A nervous knot formed in her stomach as she paced back and forth on the tiny porch.

Finally, Meg could not stand the worry that swirled inside of her. She turned the door handle and the door swung open easily. It was dark and warm inside. The shades were drawn and Mrs. Storm was still curled in a ball on the couch. Meg felt perspiration begin to bead on her forehead. What if Mrs. Storm was . . . was . . . Oh, she just *had* to be okay, Meg told herself.

Meg bent over Mrs. Storm. The older woman's eyes were closed and her hair was a mass of tangled grey curls that fell over her face. Worst of all was the way Mrs. Storm looked. Her face had a grey cast to it, unlike anything Meg had ever seen. But Mrs. Storm *was* breathing. Her breath wheezed in and out in powerful gulps.

Meg shook her friend gently, but the older woman did not stir. Her arm was hot, and when Meg laid a hand across her forehead it was even hotter, almost like it was on fire.

She's really sick, Meg realized, wishing she had told someone on Saturday that Mrs. Storm was sick. Inside, Meg squirmed. *She needs help,* she thought.

Meg pulled the blankets up over Mrs. Storm's tiny form and spun around. She dashed out the door, slowing only to shut it behind her. Then she ran down the path for help.

By the time Dad had summoned the ambulance and Mrs. Storm had been whisked away, Meg was drained. She sank down on a chair in the living room, feeling as if a heavy weight were pressing in on her from all sides. Mrs. Storm was very sick, they'd told her. Very sick. A tear slid down Meg's cheek as memories flashed through her mind. She remembered the first time she had held a nut out to a squirrel and he had taken it right from her fingers and scurried away with it. It was Mrs. Storm who had showed Meg how to get the squirrel to trust her that much. The first time she'd seen a doe and its fawn walk across the clearing also came to mind. The doe had taken an apple from the stump where Mrs. Storm had placed it earlier that day. Together, Meg and Mrs. Storm had watched the doe from the cottage window. Then Mrs. Storm had pulled out paper and pencil and shown Meg how to draw the doe. Meg could still see the picture in her mind. Mrs. Storm's sketches always came to life on the page, and this one had been no different. Mrs. Storm had taught Meg how to draw a deer, but Meg's sketches still did not have that kind of life.

Meg felt her mom beside her. Two arms surrounded Meg as Mom pulled her close. "Why don't you go out and see the new colt?" Mom suggested. "He is so pretty and full of life, and I think that is just what you need right now."

Meg rose halfheartedly. She nodded

and tried to smile, but all she could think about was Mrs. Storm. Slowly, she walked to the barn, her head held low. When she heard Foxy whinny, she looked up. Foxy stretched her long red neck over the gate and rattled the latch as she begged for a treat. Meg couldn't help but smile through her sadness. Then she saw Azure hiding behind the mare's legs. Peeking through the strands of his mother's tail, he softly gazed at Meg.

Meg went into the barn and came out with a handful of oats. As Foxy's soft lips lifted them from her palm, Azure scooted out from behind his mother and came to greet Meg.

Meg crawled through the fence bars and held a hand out to the foal. His blue eyes were still startling to her, but his look was a comical one, full of curiosity and newfound trust. As Foxy wandered toward the stall door, Azure came to Meg, moving in a stiff-legged hop as if he wanted to play. Meg felt the joy of having Azure mingle with the pain of worry that was lodged in her heart. She moved toward the foal and wrapped her arms around his neck. He stood still, whuffing soft breaths into her hair and down her neck as she let her emotions spill out. His furry neck caught her tears.

That night Meg slept fitfully. The dreams of magical horses came to her again, and she heard the stallion calling clearly from the mountaintop. His bugle sounded like a song, the tones floating on the wind like musical notes.

When she awoke on Tuesday morning, Meg wondered if the dreams were truly dreams. They had seemed so real. Especially the sound of the stallion's call.

Meg wandered outside where she found the colt sleeping with his mother under the flowering apple tree. When Meg opened the gate, Azure scrambled to his hooves while Foxy rose lazily, shaking the blossoms from her mane. Meg was amazed to see Azure racing in circles around his mother.

Meg approached the young colt, expecting him to dash off, but he came to her willingly, nudging his head in under her arm, playfully pulling on the hem of her T-shirt with straight, white teeth.

"Oh, you silly Azure," Meg said, rubbing the fluff of his mane gently.

She felt a push from behind and turned to see Foxy. *Careful with my baby boy,* Foxy said as clearly as if the words had been spoken. Meg stared at Foxy briefly. Okay, she told herself. I should be used to this by now. Turning to Foxy, she raised the mare's head and kissed her on the star right in the middle of her forehead. "I wish I knew when you learned how to do that," she said out loud, "and how!"

Foxy snorted in answer and strode over to the water bucket. She lowered her head and drank, pulling long, cool gulps of water from the bucket.

Meg watched the mare a moment, reveling in the way the rays of morning sun lit her coat and turned it a fiery red. Then Meg turned back to the newborn. She rubbed a hand over the ridge of his tiny back, losing her fingers in the thick baby fur. She ran a fingertip down the nose and knelt to place a kiss on the tip of Azure's whiskery muzzle. She rubbed the fuzzy fringe that would grow to become a mane, and slipped her hand under the forelock to scratch—and that is when she felt it.

Meg lifted the forelock to look. An angry-looking lump, almost the size of a golf ball, swelled under Meg's fingertips. Meg gasped and closed her eyes, feeling tears rise behind the eyelids. *My perfect foal,* she thought. *What is wrong with Azure?*

6

Dr. Shura came the next day, but not before Meg had spent what seemed like half the day pacing back and forth from the kitchen to the dining room, and in and out to the barn and back several times to check and recheck Azure.

The young colt took it all in stride. He only stopped frolicking long enough to get a rubdown and to question Meg with those intense blue eyes of his. But Meg couldn't tell the colt or his mother about the lump. So she blinked back tears and waited.

Inside the house, Dad waited with Meg. She was happy that he could change his hours at work just to be with her. As manager and part-owner of Fishy's Bait and Tackle Shop Dad could vary his hours, and Meg was glad.

It was lunchtime when Dr. Shura finally pulled into the driveway, her silver truck glistening in the bright noon sun. Meg ran to meet her.

"How is that newborn doing?" Dr. Shura asked. Pulling a big black bag from the back of the truck, she rattled and clanked her supplies so loudly that she didn't hear Meg's reply. "I meant to stop by and see him yesterday," Dr. Shura said as she pulled her hand from the back of the truck and slammed the door shut. "The time just got away from me." She paused. "How old is he now . . . a week?"

Meg nodded.

The back door banged on its hinges and Mom and Dad came out. "So, how are they doing?" the veterinarian repeated her question.

"I'm not sure," Dad said, and the worry reflected in his voice.

Dr. Shura set her bag down and

brushed a long, red curl from her eyes. A look of concern crossed over her face. "Is something wrong, Jim?"

"The colt is just lovely," Mom said. "Pure white, with big blue eyes!"

"Ah," Dr. Shura sighed. "Moon-eyed. They say a foal with moon eyes is easy to train and good-natured. Good luck, too!"

"But there is something," Dad said. He rubbed a hand through his short hair.

Meg felt like she was going to explode inside. Why did adults always do this? *It takes a kid to get to the point,* she thought.

"He has a lump!" Meg finally blurted out. "A big lump, under his forelock!"

Except for the crunching of gravel underfoot as they walked toward the barn, there was silence. Meg couldn't help but think that Mrs. Storm would know just which questions to ask, if she were here.

Finally, Dr. Shura tousled Meg's hair. "Well, let's have a look," she said at last. "Whatever it is, we'll take care of it."

Foxy was grazing in the far corner of the pasture, but when Dad let loose with a piercing whistle, she came cantering down the slope. Azure darted back and forth just behind her, a blur of white.

Dr. Shura smiled. "He certainly looks healthy enough," she said. "What a beauty!" she added as the foal slid to a stop in front of her.

Foxy slipped her nose over the fence, rooting in Meg's outstretched hands for a treat. When she found none she wandered into her stall, then out again; but Azure stayed, staring expectantly at Meg.

Meg could barely stand to look at the colt, she was so sure he would see the sadness in her eyes. She rubbed his neck through the fence rails as Dr. Shura and Dad opened the gate and went inside.

Dr. Shura lifted the forelock away from the young foal's head and examined the lump. Although it was covered with thin, white hair, it still looked terrible to Meg. *Is it bigger?* she asked herself. *No, it's only my imagination.*

The veterinarian felt the lump, pressing it from side to side. Azure didn't seem

to mind. He lowered his head as if the doctor were giving him a generous scratching. "Hmmm," Dr. Shura uttered. "Hmmm. It doesn't seem to hurt the fella."

"His name is Azure," Meg offered.

"What a nice name," Dr. Shura stopped her examination and looked into the colt's eyes. "Especially with those blues," she added.

After listening to his chest, taking his temperature, checking his teeth and hooves, and having a final look at the lump, Dr. Shura released Azure, closed her bag, and stepped out of the pasture.

"I can't tell you what it is," she said softly. "I've never before seen anything like it on a horse. The lump doesn't move. It isn't inflamed or sore. In fact, Azure seemed to like me rubbing it."

Mom had watched everything quietly up until now. "What should we do?" she asked. "What if it is serious?"

"I don't think it is," Dr. Shura intoned. "But just to be on the safe side, I could X-ray it."

"Can we make an appointment?" Dad asked.

Dr. Shura smiled. "We can do it today, if you like. I have a portable X ray in the truck."

"Oh! I didn't know it would be that easy. Let's do it, then!" Dad rubbed his hands together. "The sooner we know, the better."

It only took Dr. Shura a minute to return with the portable X-ray machine from her truck. Dr. Shura gave each of them a lead vest to wear for the procedure. "This will protect us from the effects of the X ray," she told Meg as she slipped a vest on too.

Dad held Azure's halter.

"Easy, boy," Meg whispered, her arms wrapped around the colt's tiny neck. The foal stared at her as if to say, *But of course,* and stood quietly, his clear gaze focused straight ahead. The only part of him to move was his ears. They twitched back and forth as Meg whispered soft reassurances behind him.

Mom helped Dr. Shura by holding the flat

film box on one side of the foal's head. Dr. Shura ran a wand-like instrument over the opposite side of the foal's face. A moment later, she straightened up and smiled briefly. "That should do it," she said, tucking the equipment back into its case.

"I'll take this film in to be developed and get back to you sometime tomorrow."

As Dad and Mom followed Dr. Shura from the pasture, Meg rubbed the colt's neck with affection. "It'll be all right," she told Azure. "You'll be fine."

Azure stretched his neck up until he reached his full height, and gazed at her haughtily. *But of course I will,* his eyes said, and he strutted up the field toward his mother, walking purposefully, his head and tail held with pride.

Meg watched him go, feeling confused. *How did he do that?* she wondered. *How did he and Foxy make her feel like they were really talking? And why didn't they do it to Mom and Dad?*

Walking back to the house, Meg shook her head in wonder. There was something special about Azure. Something different. But she didn't know what it was. He had a strength that other horses didn't have.

Still, she was worried. What if Azure had a tumor? What if the growth became infected? The possibility of something horrible happening frightened her. Already, she loved the colt even more than she had the first moment she had seen him. But in her mind, she could see the lump protruding from under his forelock, and it scared her.

And then, there was Mrs. Storm. Mom had said she was doing better today, but Meg had never seen her older friend get sick. *What Dad always says is right,* Meg thought angrily. *When it rains . . . it pours.*

7

The white horse came to Meg again in her dreams that night, and this time she knew that it was Azure. Even though he was older and surer, a grown-up version of her colt, she knew that it was him. He came cantering from the upper part of his pasture, a blur of white. Meg felt herself standing beside the barn. She was calling to him, but she didn't make a sound. Her words came through her eyes, and Azure answered her in the same manner.

You are magical, Meg said to Azure. *You possess powers that other horses don't. What gives you these powers?*

Meg, you are so wise, Azure answered.

The power comes from my father, the stallion on the mountain. One day he will come to you and you will see.

The sunlight pouring through the window washed over Meg's face, pulling her from the dream. As sleep left her, Meg's eyes fluttered open and the dream was gone. In its place was her bedroom, white with morning light. Meg felt the chills race up her arms and then her legs. A tingling sensation remained in her shoulder and upper thigh, and she rubbed it until it was gone. It had all seemed so real.

After washing her face and brushing her teeth, Meg pulled on a T-shirt and shorts and slipped down the stairs. She ran a comb through her hair as she went. The house was empty and the clock read 10 A.M. She had overslept.

Dad was in the barn, forking hay to the ponies. "Hey, Meggie," he said. "I didn't think you would ever get up! I did your barn chores for you. The ponies were hungry!"

Meg grinned sheepishly. "Thanks, Dad." She saw Foxy and Azure in the upper pasture grazing on tall shoots of clover and crabgrass. "Did Dr. Shura call yet?"

Dad shook his head and bent down to scrub out the water buckets and refill them.

Dr. Shura hadn't called. It would be another day of worry, Meg knew, unless she found something to occupy her time.

As if reading her thoughts, Dad straightened and made a suggestion. "Why don't you start haltertraining Azure? He needs to learn to lead while he's young. If you wait too long, he'll be too strong to wrestle with."

"Good idea!" Meg answered. In the barn, she found the tiny leather halter Dad had bought at the feed store the day they had found out that Foxy was going to have a foal. She slung it over her shoulder with a lead shank and walked toward the mare and her colt. As soon as Azure saw her approaching, he came racing down the field, sliding to a stop in front of her.

"Good morning, Azure," she said, and he answered her in the same formal manner.

Good morning, Meg, he seemed to say through those enormous blue eyes.

Meg slid a hand under his forelock to check the lump. It felt exactly the same to Meg. No larger. No smaller.

"Meggie." Dad's voice was carried up the pasture on the warm summer breeze.

"Yes?"

"I'm going in now. If you need help with Azure, give me a holler."

"Okay, I will," Meg answered. As Dad swung the gate shut and started to walk toward the house, she held the halter up to show Azure. "This is for you," she said. "It is time to halterbreak you."

Halterbreak?

"Yes. This goes on your head," she said, holding the halter up to show him again. "Then, I hook the lead shank to it and I can lead you around." She showed him the blue and white braided shank with the hook on the end.

But you don't need that! Azure said

with surprise. *I will go anywhere you want without those contraptions on my head!*

"You will?"

Azure nodded his head ever so slightly, blue eyes focused earnestly on Meg.

"But others expect you to be on a lead," Meg explained. "I couldn't take you to a show without a lead, or anywhere else away from home."

But of course you could! Azure protested.

"No. I couldn't. There are rules."

I don't think I like rules! Azure said, and anger danced in his eyes. He pawed the ground to show Meg that he was serious.

"Just let me put the halter on you," she said. "Just see if you mind it? Your mother wears one."

Azure turned his head to look at his mother, who was still grazing in the upper pasture, then he lowered his head. *I guess I'll try it,* he answered slowly.

Meg slid the halter on over his ears, gently avoiding the lump on the colt's forehead. She buckled the thin strap below his jaw.

Azure shook his head. His mane and forelock danced and the halter clanked softly.

Azure rolled his eyes with frustration and the whites showed clearly around the edges. *Remove it!* he demanded, pawing the dirt with his tiny yellow hoof again.

"Just let me try the lead shank," Meg said. She reached out to clip the shank to his halter, but Azure pranced backward. Then he took off in a blaze of white, galloping down the field, sidestepping and kicking up his back hooves. He raced past the open barn door and circled back around the pasture. Kicking up the dust, he whirled past Meg and back down the pasture a second time.

All at once, a shrill neigh rang out from atop Sidling Mountain. A chill crept up Meg's spine. She had never heard the stallion's call, but she knew it from her dreams.

Azure turned his head toward the

mountain to listen, sidestepping as he ran, a tiny answering nicker escaping from him. Meg watched him and she felt a scream freeze in her throat for a second before it was released.

"AZURE!" she screamed, but her words did not come in time. With his head turned and his eyes on the mountain, Azure slammed into the open stall door, shoulder first. Upon impact the colt bounced backwards, collapsing in a bundle of white.

Meg felt her heart racing—throbbing in her chest and throat—as she ran toward the barn. Azure was struggling to rise, not unlike the day of his birth. By the time Meg reached him he was on his feet, head hanging, sides trembling. A deep gash ran down his chest at an angle, crossing onto his shoulder. The blood ran crimson against his pure white body.

8

Meg ran to Azure. She must have called out as she ran, although she couldn't remember doing it. But Dad had heard her. He leapt the fence and was beside Meg and Azure in less than a moment.

Azure looked up at Meg with pain etching his eyes. Meg felt the guilt wash over her. A bitter taste rose in her throat as she removed the halter—the "contraption" Azure had not wanted to wear! If only she had heeded his wishes. . . .

The cut was deep, a long slash which had let loose a gush of blood upon impact, but barely trickled now. After Dad examined Azure, Meg ran clear water from the hose over the wound to cleanse it. Azure stood still, watching, his face expression-less. When Meg finished washing the wound, Dad locked the colt and his mother in the barn surrounded by fresh straw, and went to the house to call Dr. Shura.

Meg rubbed Azure's neck. "I'm so sorry," she said softly. "I am so, so sorry!"

Foxy pushed her son close with her nose, nudging his body sideways until it rested against hers and he began to nurse. Meg watched them for a moment. They were lost in a world of their own, one which did not include Meg; so she slipped from the barn, leaving the two alone.

Inside, Mom, Dad, and Meg sat at the kitchen table, waiting again. "It has been one thing after another," Dad said.

Meg's head drooped until her chin practically rested on her chest. It was all her fault. She knew it was. If she hadn't insisted on making Azure wear the halter and lead shank, the colt would never have dashed off like he had.

"You mustn't blame yourself," Dad said. "Accidents happen." But his voice lacked conviction, and Meg's guilt seemed like more than she could bear.

By evening Dr. Shura was back at the farm again. She didn't have the results from the X ray, a fact which only added to Meg's worry.

"It's a clean cut," Dr. Shura said. She tousled Meg's hair in what Meg knew was an attempt to reassure her, but the guilt had already settled in her stomach like an undigested cucumber. It was a lump that could not be cured with pills or reassurances. It was a lump that Meg felt she deserved to carry for a lifetime.

After putting a few tiny butterfly stitches over the cut, Dr. Shura left a spray antiseptic and instructions to clean and then spray the wound three times a day for the next week.

"Tomorrow we'll have the X-ray results," she promised Meg as she left. Her parting words to Meg were, "Don't worry!"

Easier said than done, Meg thought with a grimace. By then, she felt as though she were worn so thin that her inside seams might just burst. She felt tears threatening, and she excused herself to go to bed.

The next day, Meg overslept again. It wasn't until her mother shook her awake that she finally rolled out of bed.

"Mrs. Storm is home from the hospital," Mom said cheerfully. "Maybe you'd like to pay her a visit?"

Meg nodded sleepily, then stood. "How is she?" she asked.

Mom took Meg's hand and pulled her down as she sat on the unmade bed. "I'm afraid she is not well yet. But she is better than she was."

"Then why is she home already?" Meg asked. "She was only in the hospital for two days!" She wanted her friend home from the hospital, but she realized that she wanted her *well* even more.

"She insisted," Mom said slowly. "She just would not stay. She said she couldn't get well unless she was home, in her own bed." Mom stood again, pulling Meg back to her feet. "That's another reason I'd like to see you pay her a visit," Mom said. "Let's keep an eye on her as much as we can."

Mrs. Storm was sitting in her over-stuffed chair, gazing out the window into the garden, when Meg arrived. She went to the older woman and wrapped her arms around her neck.

"I missed you," Meg said as she sank into a chair beside Mrs. Storm.

At first, Mrs. Storm did not look up. She just continued to stare out the window. Meg ducked her head low to look out the windowpane. She could see two shiny red apples sitting on the feeding stump. Had Mrs. Storm gone outside, as sick as she was, to leave apples on the stump? Meg wondered.

"I missed you too, honey." Mrs. Storm's voice finally quivered with an answer. Each breath came wrapped in a coarse, wheezy whistle. The sound sent a shiver

up Meg's spine. A warning bell rang in her head. Mrs. Storm was still very sick!

"A lot happened while you were in the hospital," Meg blurted out nervously. Then she told Mrs. Storm about her beautiful colt, and the lump, and his accident, and by the time she was through, Meg felt weak and tired, too.

Mrs. Storm listened with a faraway look in her eyes. Then she smiled. "Just like his father," she said so low that Meg had to bend her head to hear the words.

"What do you mean?" Meg asked.

All at once Mrs. Storm straightened in her chair, and her eyes focused clearly on Meg. "Nothing," she said. "Nothing at all. Just the ramblings of an old woman. But don't you worry about that foal," she added strongly. "He will be better quicker than you can guess. Same as I will. The stallion takes care of those he loves." She paused. "Like me," Meg thought she heard Mrs. Storm add.

Meg looked sharply at Mrs. Storm, but the woman's eyes were unfocused again, looking for something outside the window. What does that mean? Meg wondered. *The stallion takes care of those he loves.*

During the evening hours, Meg curled up in the big rocking chair in the living room, pretending to read a book. What she was really doing, though, was thinking and worrying—puzzling over Mrs. Storm's strange words, and worrying about both the colt and her older friend. Meg felt as if she were living in a dream. Why had she so easily believed in the way the colt and his mother spoke to her through their eyes? She had long ago lost her faith in magic, yet lately she believed in it more strongly than she ever had before. But something somewhere deep inside her told her that she must keep quiet about it. The magic was not for just anyone. After all, Foxy had not spoken to Mom, or Dad, or Dr. Shura, or anyone else! *Yes,* she thought. *The magic is meant for me and no one else.* But she did not know why, or what would happen next.

9

Meg tossed and turned in her bed, too
tired to open her eyes, too worried to
sleep. Mrs. Storm did not seem much
better than when she had gone to the
hospital. Yet she had been well enough
to carry two apples out to her feeding
stump. Meg didn't know what to make
of it, or of the strange things Mrs.
Storm had said about the stallion. Meg
rolled onto her side and threw her blankets off.

It was almost a relief when she heard
the stallion call. His whinny seemed
more clear and urgent than she had ever
heard it before. Rising, Meg padded to
the window. Crumpling to her knees with

exhaustion, she rested her chin on the windowsill and watched. A full moon spilled light over the backyard, almost as bright as day.

Foxy's head was hanging out over the stall's half-door. Her nostrils quivered in the sharp moonlight, and her answering call rang out.

Meg heard hoofbeats coming down the mountain, and she thought she saw a flash of white in the shadowy trees, but then the night fell silent. Meg waited for the stallion to call again.

Meg awoke wet with sweat, her face sticking to the wide wooden sill. She lifted her head and rubbed sleep from her eyes. Then she remembered. She had fallen asleep waiting for the stallion to show himself. Had he come to the barn to see Foxy and Azure as she slept? she wondered. Had he seen what she had done to his son?

The lump in Meg's stomach was still there, just as it had been the night before. "Oh, Azure," she sighed out loud.

Meg didn't bother to comb her hair or brush her teeth. She saw the shorts and T-shirt she had worn the night before. Dirty and crumpled, they lay in a pile on the floor. Shrugging, she slipped the shorts on under her nightgown, then traded her nightgown for the dirty T-shirt and headed down the steps.

She realized when she reached the empty kitchen that it was still early. The clock read 6 A.M. and the light that filtered in through the gauzy curtains was not full; but Mom was already in the kitchen.

"Mrs. Storm called this morning," Mom told Meg.

"Mrs. Storm!" Meg answered quickly. "This early . . . what's wrong?"

"Nothing is wrong, Meg," Mom said. "She sounded just wonderful. She said she knew I'd be up, and she wanted to let us know that she was better."

"But she was so sick just yesterday . . ."

"I know. That's what I thought, but she sounded wonderful," Mom said, smiling. "She sounded just like her old self again.

Just the same, maybe you could pay her a visit, just to see," she added.

Meg shook her head in agreement. "I'll go see her today!" She gulped down half a glass of tomato juice and wandered outside to see the ponies.

Foxy was lying on her side in the straw. Azure was resting against her, his shoulder and back leaning on her belly, his neck and head draped across her front legs. Meg watched them sleep. Their breathing caused their sides to rise and fall softly; Azure's in quick succession, Foxy's slower and more rhythmic.

From where Meg stood peering over the stall's half-door, Foxy and Azure looked like two perfectly normal ponies, a mother and her foal resting in a bed of yellow straw. But Meg knew they were not normal. They were filled with a kindness she had never seen in any animal before, and they spoke without talking. *Somewhere on her journey,* Meg thought, *Foxy met up with magic, and she carried it home with her, and passed it on to her son, too.*

She could not see Azure's wounded shoulder. She could not see the angry bump that had sprung from his forehead just after birth. But try as she might, Meg could not forget that they existed.

Meg swallowed the lump that had risen in her throat and forced herself to be calm and quiet. But it was too late. Foxy and Azure had heard her. They blinked their eyes rapidly as they became used to the light of day. Foxy pushed her son gently and he stretched out on the straw, leaving the comfort of her side. Foxy rose and shook the straw from her red coat, then stuck her head over the door, nudging Meg roughly.

Meg looked at her pony with love and the pony looked back. *Don't worry, Meg,* she said with soft brown eyes. *Azure is fine!*

Meg rubbed her pony's neck sorrowfully. She felt Foxy's velvety muzzle slip into her palm, and it calmed her. Meg bent to kiss the snip of white on the top of Foxy's warm muzzle. As she did, Azure rose and came to stand beside his mother.

"Hi, boy," Meg said quietly. "How do you feel today?"

Azure sidled closer to the door, crowding his mother as he stretched his neck up to Meg. *I am well,* he said. His blue eyes looked into Meg's own, and they seemed to reach beyond and into her soul. *You needn't worry,* he said with a gentleness that Meg could not understand. *I really am fine!*

"Well, let's have a look at the cut," she said. "The doctor says I have to wash it out and spray it with medicine."

There is no need for that, Azure said.

Meg swallowed hard. She didn't expect another battle so soon today. Should she listen to Azure? she wondered. Should she do what *he* wanted, or what the doctor had told her to do? Meg fought down the swirl of arguments that were rising inside of her. If only she had listened to Azure in the first place, he wouldn't have been hurt.

He is smart, she told herself. Maybe I should listen to him.

But he needs to heal, another part of her said. Meg lowered her head and rested her chin on the stall door, miserable.

Meg! The voice that rang out was clear and firm. *Listen to my son. There is no need to worry. He is fine!*

Meg lifted her head and slid back the latch on the door. Swinging the door wide, she watched as Foxy strode from the stall, followed by Azure. He trotted out quickly, right smack on Foxy's tail. Then he darted into the field, stretching his legs in a leisurely canter.

Meg watched him move. There was no stiffness in his gait! It was as smooth as glazed honey. His eyes were bright with color, and he looked happy. He was not the miserable, injured foal she had left in the stall the night before.

As she watched him, Azure rounded the field and cantered toward her. Sliding to a stop, he sniffed her hand, looking for a treat.

"I'm sorry, boy," she said. "I didn't know you would be feeling well enough to eat!"

Azure gazed at Meg, then ran his muzzle up and down her arm with a caress. *I am fine, Meg,* Azure said. *Just look and see!* Quickly, Azure swung his body sideways so that Meg could see the shoulder that had been injured. Meg looked at the place where his wound should have been, then blinked hard.

"Where's the cut?" she wondered out loud. Confusion filled her as Meg fell to her knees in front of the colt. She threw her arms around his tiny neck and rested her face in the warm white coat. "Oh, Azure, you *are* well! But how?"

Azure bowed his head, breathing softly into Meg's curls, tickling her neck with his breaths. *My father came,* he said simply. *My father, the stallion, healed my cut.*

Later that evening, Meg hurried through the forest to visit with Mrs. Storm. She found her friend snipping lilacs from a large bush with a pair of pruning shears. The sweet scent of lilacs filled the air, and the sweetness of Mrs. Storm's smile filled Meg.

"You're really alright!" she said in wonder.

"Yes," Mrs. Storm said. "I am fine, just as I said I would be. My friend came and made me well."

10

Meg rested, stomach-down on her bed. The wonder of Azure's healing had been a lot to adjust to. And then there was the matter of Mrs. Storm getting well so quickly. Meg wondered who Mrs. Storm's mysterious friend could be. She sighed. So much had happened since Azure's birth just three weeks ago. So much.

Meg closed her eyes and tried to picture Azure's father. He was white. She knew that, for she had not only seen him in her dreams, but also through the shadowy trees at night. What kind of horse had healing powers? Meg wondered. What kind of horse came and went at will, as wild and free as the mountain breezes and the moon that drifted aimlessly across the skies at night? Where did the stallion come from? As she pondered all of these questions, Meg's eyes drifted shut and she fell into a fitful sleep.

"Meg!" Meg raised her head from her mattress, surprised that she had actually slept in the middle of the day.

"Meg! Dr. Shura is here to see the colt!"

Meg leapt from her bed, her head spinning as she dashed down the stairs, still full of the webs of sleep and half-dreams.

As she neared the living room, Meg heard Dad's deep voice. "You won't believe it when you see the colt. His cut is already healed!"

Meg quickened her pace, hearing Dr. Shura's answering voice. "Often a cut looks like it is healed long before it actually is," she said cheerily. "Let me have a look at it. I'm sure it has a way to go before it is completely healed."

Meg burst into the room, breathless from her dash down the stairs. "It really has healed!" she said.

As they walked toward the barn together, Dr. Shura stopped at her truck. "I want you to have a look at these," she said, pulling several large but flimsy sheets from an envelope. They looked like photographic negatives to Meg.

"These are Azure's X rays," Dr. Shura explained. Holding them up to the light, she squinted and traced the rough outline of Azure's head with a fingertip. "This is his forehead," she said, "and this is the lump." Her finger was resting on a white spot in the X ray. "The bump appears to be a deposit of calcium."

At Meg's puzzled look, she slid the pictures into the envelope and continued. "Calcium is bone," she explained. "For some unknown reason, Azure has a bump made of bone. I don't think it's anything to worry about," she added. "I would just leave it alone for now. It will probably stay like that forever."

Azure whinnied and came trotting to greet them when they reached the barn. Dr. Shura knelt to examine his chest and shoulder, and Meg saw the look of astonishment that crossed her face as she touched the spot where the deep cut had once been.

"You're right," she said slowly, a tremor in her voice. "It *has* healed! In all my years of practicing medicine for animals, I have never seen a cut heal this fast. It's almost like magic."

After Dr. Shura left, Meg stayed with the ponies. She played tag with the young colt, racing up and down the field. Azure reared on his hind legs like a big stallion, dancing down the pasture. He sidestepped like a crab and played tag like a kid. Meg realized that she had come to love him, just as she loved her foxy pony.

Meg's nightgown swooshed about her legs as she slipped down the darkened stairs, as quietly as the clouds that slid across the moonlit sky just outside the window. Meg opened the door, flinched at the squeak of rusty hinges, then closed it quickly behind her.

The moon hung low in the sky as she silently crossed the backyard to the barn. She had seen the yearning in Foxy's eyes earlier in the day. That was when she knew that the stallion would come again. This time she knew that she had to meet him, to see him for herself . . . even if it meant waiting all night.

A tiny nicker rang out when Azure saw

her coming. He shoved his nose through the rails, nudging her gently as she climbed between them and into the pasture. He had grown so strong in the month since his birth. Feeling her way along the side of the barn, Meg headed toward the stall. Peering through the doorway, up into the dark foothills, she saw Foxy's head held high.

Suddenly Meg's leg hit the edge of the water bucket. Her foot slid sideways and she went down on one knee. A stone cut the skin and a tiny trickle of blood surfaced.

Brushing it away impatiently, Meg felt her way into the stall. She turned the empty feed bucket upside down and sat on it in the doorway of the barn as Foxy left the barn to graze in the pasture.

The burning sensation in Meg's knee brought tears to her eyes, but she rubbed them away as quickly as she'd rubbed the blood from her scraped knee. She squinted into the dark, hearing the eery *Whooo, Whooo* of an owl float down from the locust tree nearby.

Azure wandered away, grabbing mouthfuls of grass as he walked. Every now and then he would raise his head, prick his ears, and stare expectantly into the hills.

The chirping tree frogs and crickets lulled Meg and her eyelids soon drifted shut.

All at once Meg opened her eyes. There was a heavy feeling in the air and silence all around. As her eyes readjusted to the moonlight, Meg searched the pasture for Azure and Foxy.

Then she saw the stallion. He emerged from a cluster of trees near the hedgerow, his neck arched gracefully, his mane falling in waves from his neck, and his tail splashing the ground with silky white. Foxy moved to greet him, stretching her neck upward. She squealed with delight as his nose touched hers.

Meg felt the breath catch in her throat as she watched the stallion turn away. His muscles rippled with power as he strode toward the barn, moonlight and trees checkering his pure white body with shadows.

Meg froze in her spot on the overturned water bucket. She was afraid. The stallion was tall and powerful . . . and she was alone.

He moved away from the hedgerow, stepping into the center of the pasture. Moonlight flooded over him like water cascading over a statue of gold and pearls, glistening white. Meg gasped. The stallion was gorgeous, but that was not why she gasped. A single horn twisted from the center of his forehead in a golden spiral.

He's a unicorn, Meg thought with amazement; yet deep in her heart, she knew that she had known all along. The thought had barely materialized when the stallion strode toward her. Meg scrunched into the shadows as he flowed across the field, all ripples and sparkles. Meg quivered, but stayed frozen to the water bucket as the stallion approached.

Meg's heart raced wildly when he stopped in front of her. Slowly, he lowered his head, his muzzle brushing her forehead in a velvety soft kiss. Then, he

lowered his horn to her knee, and the burning stopped. When he lifted his head, the scrape was gone! It had healed with the touch of his horn!

Suddenly, Meg knew how Mrs. Storm had become well overnight . . . and why she had demanded to come home to heal, and had placed the apples on the stump.

Meg turned to call for Azure, her heart brimming over with emotion. Azure came quickly, trotting down the fence line. He stopped in front of Meg and pawed the ground, lowering his head to Meg just as his father had done. Moonlight glistened off the tiny golden horn that now sprouted from the young unicorn's head.

"Oh, Azure," Meg said lovingly, and she buried her head into the warm, white fuzz of her young unicorn's neck. "Mrs. Storm was right," Meg whispered huskily. "When she said that the stallion takes care of those he loves, she was right."

Meg released Azure then, and the two of them followed the dancing shadow of the white stallion until he leapt the fence. They watched the shadowy form melt into the dark, checkered bushes.

Meg thought of how she, and Mrs. Storm, and even Foxy had been touched by magic, and how it had made everything in life possible. She watched Foxy and Azure. Their eyes were still on the hills, their nostrils flared wide. A moment later, Foxy wandered away to lip up grass in the light of the moon. But Azure kept his eyes trained on the hillside. He had not been simply touched by magic. He, like his father . . . *was* magic.

Meg slipped an arm around Azure's neck and hugged him close. She did it for all the times she would not be able to do it in the future. She did it because she knew that one day he would sail over the fence, and follow his father the stallion into the hills, to spread magic.

Look for all the stories about horses . . .
by Lois Szymanski

A PERFECT PONY
78267-7/$3.99 US/$4.99 Can

At the horse auction, Niki sees a beautiful white mare that's perfect for her. But then she spots a little black horse with spindley legs and big sad eyes, and Niki must decide whether to bid for her "perfect" pony with her head . . . or her heart.

And Don't Miss

A PONY PROMISE
78266-9/$3.99 US/ $5.50 Can

LITTLE ICICLE
77567-0/$3.50 US/$4.50 Can

A NEW KIND OF MAGIC
77349-X/$3.50 US/$4.50 Can

PATCHES
76841-0/$3.99 US/$5.50 Can

Coming Soon

LITTLE BLUE EYES
78487-4/$3.99 US/$4.99 Can

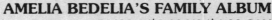
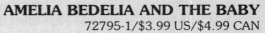

IF YOU DARE TO BE SCARED...
READ SPINETINGLERS!
by M.T. COFFIN

Read All the Stories by
Beverly Cleary

JOIN IN THE FUN IN THE WACKY WORLD OF WAYSIDE SCHOOL
by
LOUIS SACHAR

SIDEWAYS STORIES FROM WAYSIDE SCHOOL
69871-4/ $4.50 US/ $5.99 Can

Anything can happen in a school that was all mixed up from the day it was built.

WAYSIDE SCHOOL IS FALLING DOWN
75484-3/ $4.50 US/ $5.99 Can

All the kids in Miss Jewls' class help turn each day into one madcap adventure after another.

WAYSIDE SCHOOL GETS A LITTLE STRANGER
72381-6/ $4.50 US/ $5.99 Can

Also by
Louis Sachar

JOHNNY'S IN THE BASEMENT
83451-0/ $4.50 US/ $6.50 Can

SOMEDAY ANGELINE
83444-8/ $4.50 US/ $6.50 Can